TOUCHED
BY AN
ANGEL

# Have You Seen Me?

"Hey, Noah. You look just like this little kid who's lost! Look, his picture is on the milk carton."

**TOUCHED**
BY AN
**ANGEL**

# Have You Seen Me?

Written by Monica Hall
Based on a teleplay by
Pamela Redford Russell
from a story by R. J. Colleary

Martha Williamson
Executive Producer

Based on the television
series created by
John Masius

**Tommy NELSON**

Thomas Nelson, Inc.
Nashville

*Have You Seen Me?*
Book Two in the *Touched By An Angel* fiction series.

Touched By An Angel is a trademark of CBS Broadcasting Inc. Used under license.

Copyright © 1998 CBS Worldwide, Inc.

*Have You Seen Me?* by Monica Hall is based on a teleplay by Pamela Redford Russell from a story by R. J. Colleary.

Published in Nashville, Tennessee, by Tommy Nelson™, a division of Thomas Nelson, Inc. Executive Editor: Laura Minchew; Managing Editor: Beverly Phillips.

**Library of Congress Cataloging-in-Publication Data**

Hall, Monica.
　　Have you seen me? / written by Monica Hall : based on a teleplay
　by Pamela Redford Russell ; from a story by R. J. Colleary.
　　　p. cm.—(Touched by an angel)
　　Summary: Twelve-year-old Sarah's attempt to find out how her younger
brother Noah came into her family is aided by an angel named Monica.
　　ISBN 0-8499-5803-2
　　[1. Adoption—Fiction. 2. Guardian angels—Fiction. 3. Angels—
Fiction. 4. Brothers and sisters—Fiction.] I. Russell, Pamela Redford.
II. Colleary, R. J. III. Title. IV. Series.
PZ7.H14725Has　1998
[Fic]—dc21

　　　　　　　　　　　　　　　　　　　　　　　　　98-11475
　　　　　　　　　　　　　　　　　　　　　　　　　　　CIP
　　　　　　　　　　　　　　　　　　　　　　　　　　　　AC

*Printed in the United States of America*
98 99 00 01 DHC 9 8 7 6 5 4 3 2 1

# Contents

# Contents

# The Characters

**Sarah,** a bright, curious twelve-year-old, who loves mysteries—until she finds one in her own family.

**Noah,** Sarah's talented eight-year-old brother, who cheerfully puts up with a lot of sisterly teasing.

**Amy Monroe,** Sarah's loving, protective mother, who balances work and family with grace and ease—except for the cooking part!

**Jake Monroe,** Sarah's funny, understanding father, who'd do anything for his family—including half the household chores.

**Grant Abbott,** a sad, lonely man, who thinks the most precious things in his life are gone forever.

**Ray Bishop,** a nervous little man with a big secret, who learns he can't run away from the truth.

# The Characters

**Tess,** a warm, motherly angel with strong opinions about a lot of things—from music to truth. She is sent by God to help the Monroe family face both.

**Monica,** a joyful young angel with a heart as tender as her smile. She is sent by God to help Sarah find—and accept—the answers she's looking for.

**Andrew,** an angel of compassion, who never takes 'no' for an answer. He is sent by God to help two men deal with a hard truth from their past.

# Introduction

Sarah grinned to herself as she splashed the last of the milk onto her cereal: The 'Monroe Morning Ballet' was in full swing!

Jake slid the last perfect egg onto the last plate.

Amy dropped her briefcase and dashed to the smoking toaster. "Drat, Jake, I burned the toast *again!*" (Let's face it; Dad was a much better cook than Mom.)

And Noah—smart little guy—drank his orange juice and kept out of everyone's way.

Noah was Sarah's darling. Not that she'd ever tell him that. Little brothers had to be kept in their place. And she'd lose her 'Big Sister License' for sure if she didn't bug him now and then.

"We're out of milk, Mom," Sarah called, bumping Noah's elbow just a little.

"Sarah!" Noah sputtered through his juice.

"Sarah," echoed Jake and Amy, without even looking.

Swallowing her last bite of egg, Amy slipped into her bright blue real estate company blazer. "I'll get milk on the way home, honey."

"Hey, Noah," called Dad, "what do you want to do for your birthday?"

"Can I have a party?" Noah loved parties. Especially his own.

"Of course you can, pal," said Jake. "Chocolate cake again?"

Sitting at the breakfast table, two unseen visitors watched a Monroe morning unfold.

"They seem like a very happy family," said Monica.

"They are," answered Tess, ". . . for the moment."

Monica was puzzled by Tess's answer. "Are they my assignment?"

"No," said Tess, "only Sarah." She smiled tenderly at the mischievous twelve-year-old.

"Miss Curiosity over there is yours. The parents are mine."

Monica looked over at Noah. "And what about that wee boy? Whose is he?"

"That's the question, baby," Tess replied. "The question that has to be answered."

As the elevator zoomed up, Tess frowned at Andrew. He was humming along with that awful piped-in music! "I can't stand elevator music," she grumbled. Just like that—in mid-note—the music cut off. Tess lifted grateful eyes toward heaven. "Thank you," she murmured as the elevator came to a stop.

The two men who stepped in couldn't see the angels who were riding with them.

"Are these the guys?" asked Andrew.

Tess nodded, then pointed at the chunky little man who bounced impatiently from foot to foot as the elevator rose. "His name is Ray.

He needs your help to be freed from a great secret he is carrying."

"Looks like a man in a hurry," said Andrew as Ray rushed through the opening doors and zipped off down the hall. Then he looked at the slender man with the cold, sad eyes. "What about him?"

"That's Grant," Tess answered. "He has a secret, too. And more guilt than any one man deserves. He's been through some hard times. And they're about to get harder."

# Chapter One

## Puzzles and Secrets

Sarah slid onto a stool at 'Fifties,' her favorite soda shop. She was starving! Soccer practice always made her hungry. She smiled as she looked around the bright, noisy room.

Sarah loved 'Fifties'! The rainbow neon lights. The big jukebox with the old-fashioned rock-and-roll songs. The waitresses in their swingy skirts with all the petticoats—'poodle skirts,' Mom called them.

"Hello," said a friendly voice, "my name is Monica. I'll be your server today."

Sarah smiled back. "What's the special?"

Her brown eyes dancing, Monica leaned forward. "Actually," she whispered, "it isn't all that special."

Sarah laughed. "Then I guess I'll have the chocolate sundae."

"One snow-covered black cow with a siren," sang out Monica. "That'll be right up. And I'll be right back," she said, glancing at two familiar customers in the corner booth.

Andrew stretched a long arm over the back of the booth and put a quarter in the jukebox.

Quick as a flash, Tess reached over and captured one of his French fries. "Hey!" he protested.

"You looked the other way," said Tess, swallowing. "When people look the other way, they can lose a French fry . . . or they can lose something a lot more precious. Maybe even their soul." She smiled up at Monica. "Sit here, Angel Girl."

"This is going to be one nasty case," she told them. "We have six pieces to a puzzle, and we've got to make them all fit together. 'Cause we're not just talking about puzzle pieces—we're talking about six human lives."

Tess reached out and joined hands with Andrew and Monica. "Now between us we have six hands . . . and we're going to need them *all* for this case!"

# Chapter Two

## Groceries and Mysteries

Sarah sliced a tomato into the salad, sniffed the air, and smiled. It was Dad's turn to fix dinner. And tonight's 'Jake Special' smelled wonderful!

A clatter of forks announced that Noah was finished setting the table. "When's Mom coming home?"

"Any minute," said Jake. "She has a new partner, and she's showing her the ropes."

But Noah was already off on another thought. "Dad, I know what I want for my birthday."

"Great," said Jake, "what's that?"

Noah couldn't wait to tell him. "A little brother!"

"Oh, no!" gasped Sarah, clutching her throat. "No more little brothers. They're *such* a pain!"

That got an automatic "Sarah!" from Dad. But his heart wasn't in it. And he had the strangest look on his face. In fact, if this were one of her beloved mystery stories, she would have thought her dad looked like someone with something to hide. But, Dad? With a secret? No way.

Then Jake smiled at Noah. "Your mom and I aren't having any more children, son," he said quietly.

"It's not fair," said Noah. "Sarah got me!"

Sarah rolled her eyes at her father. Jake just grinned back, then hugged Noah. "Anyway, you two are all we can handle."

Noah thought it over. "Well, I either want a little brother . . . or some new paints."

Jake laughed. "Paints we can do."

"Hey, guys." Mom was home, her arms full of grocery bags, and her briefcase in one hand. And she had someone with her—a tall woman in a bright blue blazer just like her own.

"This is Tess; she's my new partner. And this," Amy told Tess with a proud smile, "is my family: Jake . . . and Sarah . . . and Noah."

Tess's smile wrapped around the Monroes like a warm hug. She shook hands with Jake, winked at Sarah, then bent down to Noah's level. "Hello there, little one."

*Little!* Noah stretched up as tall as he could. "I'm gonna be nine on Saturday!"

Tess looked impressed. "I've heard that boys are at their very smartest at age nine."

Noah grinned, then shot a 'So there!' look at Sarah.

Jake pulled a steaming pan from the oven. "Can you stay for dinner, Tess?"

Tess sniffed the spicy air. "Yes, I can," she said, "and I will."

As Sarah set another place, Amy helped Jake put dinner on the table. "Tess sold three houses on her very first day!"

Jake whistled. "Really?"

Amy nodded. "I've never seen anything like it."

Jake pulled out a chair for their guest. "Beginner's luck, huh, Tess?"

"Oh, no," she said serenely, as they bowed their heads for grace. "Not really."

Five forks dug into dinner. "Oh," said Amy, "we forgot the milk. It's in that big bag, Sarah."

But if there was milk in that grocery sack, Sarah sure couldn't find it. "Not here, Mom."

"Really?" Amy was sure she'd bought milk.

"Look under the lettuce, baby," advised Tess.

*But the lettuce is in the bottom of the bag,* thought Sarah. *Never mind, I'll look again.* And under the lettuce—exactly as Tess had said—was a carton of milk.

Funny, she was sure it hadn't been there a minute ago. As Sarah pulled it out, something caught her eye. 'Have You Seen Me?' read the message on the back of the milk carton. Underneath were two pictures: One was of a big-eyed toddler, and the other a boy of about eight—who looked kind of familiar.

Sarah knew that the second picture was made by a computer, to show how the missing boy would look today. You have to know that kind of stuff if you're going to be a detective when you grow up. And that's exactly what Sarah planned to be. Figuring things out was her specialty! She frowned at the carton. Boy, that kid sure reminded her of someone. . . .

Then she glanced at Noah's class picture on the refrigerator door. "Hey, Noah. You look just like this little kid who's lost! Look, his picture is on the milk carton."

"Sarah," sighed Jake.

"No," Sarah insisted. "I'm serious! Look."

"That's enough, Sarah." Mom was using her 'no-nonsense' voice.

"All right, all right." Sarah shrugged. Probably just her imagination—which she did have a lot of. But, of course, all the *best* detectives did!

# Chapter Three

## The Plot Thickens

Andrew was back in the elevator. *Sure are a lot of ups and downs to this job,* he thought. Then he smiled, picturing the look he'd get from Tess for such a corny joke.

*Ding.* The door slid open, and Grant Abbott stepped in.

"Good morning," Andrew said cheerfully.

But Grant just pushed the button and stared straight ahead.

Andrew tried again. "Nice day." Grant didn't answer. But Andrew wasn't ready to give up. "I'm new in the building. My name is Andrew. And you are . . . ?" he asked as the door slid open.

"I'm getting off right here," said Grant. And he did.

"Ouch," said Andrew to himself. "Strike one." Oh well, maybe he'd do better with Ray Bishop, who was just stepping in.

"Hello . . ." began Andrew.

"Hey," said Ray, beaming at Andrew like a long-lost friend. "How are you doing today, son?"

"Uh . . ." said Andrew, "I'm . . . fine . . ."

"Great, great!" broke in Ray. "Hey, that's a nice jacket. Where'd you get that? You didn't pay retail did you?"

"Um . . . I don't buy my own clothes," said Andrew. "They give them to us."

"Oh, a perk. Good, good," approved Ray. "But if you ever need something like that, I've got a guy."

"You've got . . . a guy?" Andrew was confused.

"Yeah, I've got a guy," said Ray. "You're new in the building, aren't you? I'm Ray . . . Ray Bishop. Glad to meet you."

"I'm Andrew . . ."

"If you need anything," broke in Ray, "let me know, because I've . . ."

". . . got a guy," finished Andrew.

Ray nodded. *This kid was catching on.*

"I *do* have a question . . ." Andrew began.

*Ding.* The door slid open. "Good talking to you, Andrew. See you around." And Ray bounced off down the hall.

Andrew sighed. Strike two.

Sarah tossed and turned. It was very late, but she couldn't get to sleep. Even thinking about that new mystery by her favorite writer didn't help. And Sarah loved figuring out the answer before the end of the book! But she couldn't be bothered with a made-up story tonight. She had a mystery of her own to solve . . . right here at home.

She threw back the covers, picked up her big flashlight, and crept down to the kitchen. Opening the refrigerator, she stood staring at the milk carton photo that looked so much— so very much—like Noah. But that couldn't be! Could it?

Then she shook her head, mad at herself. Detectives didn't guess. They investigated! And there *was* a way to be sure. She put back the carton and followed the dancing beam of her flashlight down the hall to the living room.

Standing on tiptoe, she could just reach the top shelf of the bookcase. There! She pulled out two photo albums. One marked 'Sarah.' One marked 'Noah.'

She looked in her book first. There she was, a tiny, wrinkled little baby in the hospital nursery. She turned a page: there she was splashing in the bath. Another page: Sarah in diapers, just learning to crawl . . . blowing out birthday candles. Page by page, Sarah watched herself grow.

Then—holding her breath—she opened Noah's book to the very first page. And stared at the picture of a smiling toddler. Quickly she flipped through the book. But Noah only got older. There were no baby pictures of her little brother!

# Chapter Four

## Missing Pieces

Noah studied Sarah with worried eyes. It wasn't every day he got clear through his cereal without a single tickle, tease, or 'hey, squirt.' "You mad at me, Sarah?" he asked.

"What?" Sarah jumped as her wandering mind came back to the busy kitchen. "No, I'm not mad." She looked at him suspiciously. "Should I be?"

Now he had her full attention.

"Hey, you haven't been in my room again have you, squirt?"

"No, no," said Noah quickly. He grinned to himself. 'Squirt.' That was more like it.

Sarah wasn't the only one with a problem to solve that morning. Andrew's problem stood waiting for the office elevator. Ray Bishop held a very important piece of this puzzle, and it was Andrew's job to help him understand that. "'Morning, Ray," he said.

"Hey, Andy," said Ray, beaming. "How're you doing?"

"I'm doing well," said Andrew. "By the way, I was wondering what kind of work you do?"

"Oh, a little of this, a little of that. How about you?" Ray answered as the elevator door opened and he stepped in.

"I thought we were talking about you," said Andrew.

"We just did," said Ray. And the door whooshed shut, leaving Andrew in the lobby.

Ray jingled the change in his pocket as the elevator rose. *Nice kid, that Andrew, but way too curious,* he thought.

*Ding.* The elevator stopped on the next floor. The door slid open. And Andrew stepped in!

"Hi, Ray."

Ray's eyes got very big. "How'd you do that?"

"Look, Ray," said Andrew, "I usually spend a lot more time on a case. But I don't have much time on this one."

Ray took a step back. "Have you escaped from somewhere?"

Andrew sighed. "You're not making this easy, Ray, so I'm just going to hit you with it all at once."

Ray jumped. "Don't touch me!" Then he blinked. Andrew was starting to . . . to . . . glow!

"I'm an angel, Ray, and God has sent me here to give you a message."

"God?" gulped Ray. "Uh-huh." And he punched every button on the panel as fast as he could.

Andrew looked him straight in the eye. "God knows what you've done, Ray. And He wants you to remember this: 'The truth will set you free.'"

As the elevator doors opened, Ray slid carefully around Andrew and ran off down the hall.

Andrew sighed as Ray darted around a corner. Then he reached out and pushed the button for Grant's floor.

"Grant doesn't come to work anymore," said a quiet voice behind him.

"Uh-oh," said Andrew.
"You said it, baby. You said it," Tess answered.

Andrew rang the doorbell to Grant's apartment. Then rang it again. And again. "Grant? Grant? Are you there?"

Grant was there. But he wasn't hearing a doorbell. Or seeing any of the beautiful paintings that lined the walls. His sad eyes were looking back into another time—a happier time that he felt was gone forever.

Instead of the brilliant swirls of joyful color that sang from the walls, Grant was seeing the artist who had created them. Jenna—beautiful Jenna—standing at her easel, smiling down at the little boy who watched her paint. Smiling that special Jenna smile. Now he'd never see her smile again.

*Buzz! Buzz!* Grant blinked and was back in his lonely apartment, his lonely life. *Buzz!* Somebody at the door. But it didn't matter. Nothing mattered.

In the hall, Andrew shook his head sadly. Grant needed more time. Andrew would come back later.

The last record spun to an end, and the juke-box lights blinked out. 'Fifties' was quiet and empty. Except for Monica, stacking chairs on tables . . . and Sarah, staring into the melted remains of her chocolate sundae.

"Closing time, Sarah," Monica called out as she gathered up dirty dishes.

Sarah didn't hear her. In fact, she hadn't heard much of anything all day—except the questions buzzing in her head.

Monica looked at her thoughtfully. "Something wrong, Sarah?"

Sarah lifted her troubled eyes. "I'm not sure what to say, or who I can say it to."

"How about your friends?" asked Monica.

Sarah shrugged. "Oh, you know, some things you can't really talk about with your friends. . . ."

"Well then," said Monica, "how about your parents?"

Sarah shook her head. "Usually, yes. This time, no."

"Well, you could talk to me if you'd like," Monica offered.

Somehow, Sarah felt she could tell Monica anything. "I saw this milk carton, you know, with the pictures of missing kids on the back? And there's this picture that looks just like . . . just like my little brother, Noah."

She waited for Monica to laugh. Or tell her it was just her imagination. But Monica surprised her. "I see. And you think it *is* Noah?"

Sarah sighed. "I don't know what to think. I checked our photo albums for his baby pictures, but there aren't any!"

Monica gave this news the serious attention it deserved. "And what do you think that means?"

"That means it's weird!" Sarah said. "But I'm not sure what *that* means."

"Does it frighten you?" Monica asked gently.

"No!" came the quick answer, followed by

the truth. "Well, maybe a little," she admitted. How she wished she knew what to do!

Monica did. "Sarah," she said briskly, "go home, tell your parents how you feel, and see what they say."

Sarah raised hopeful eyes. "You think so?" She had always been able to talk to her parents about anything. But this?

"Yes, I do," said Monica with an encouraging smile. "Go on now, I have to clean up and lock up."

"I could help you," said Sarah, hoping to delay what was coming.

"You're sweet," said Monica, "but I'll have it done in no time."

As Monica unlocked the door for her, Sarah turned around. "Are you sure I can't help you clean up?"

Monica smiled. "I'm sure."

"Well . . . good-bye, Monica."

# Chapter Five

## Suspicions and Discoveries

**B**ackpack in place, Sarah started down the stairs, then stopped, as she did every morning, on the third step down. Yes, there it was: her own personal rainbow. She smiled at the flickers of color on the wall, as sunlight streamed through the crystal hanging in the hall. 'Suncatcher.' What a perfect name!

*Thump.* Noah dropped his books on the bottom step and bent to retie his left shoe. He and Dad were deep in birthday plans.

"So," asked Jake, "what kind of party do you want?"

Noah knew exactly. "The kind where I get presents!"

Jake grinned. "That's my favorite kind, too."

Sarah took a deep breath and came down the stairs. Scooping up Noah's books, she put them in his arms. "Get lost, squirt."

"Sarah," said Dad, "be nice."

Sarah gave a long-suffering sigh. "Sorry. Get lost, squirt, *please.*"

Noah stuck out his tongue and scooted off down the hall.

"Dad?" Sarah fiddled with the zipper on her jacket. "I need some help with a school project."

"Sure, honey," said Jake. "What can I do?"

Sarah hoped God would understand why she was 'stretching' the truth. "I have to do a family tree, and I need baby pictures of everybody."

Jake smiled. "That shouldn't be too tough."

"I can find everybody except Noah."

"Noah?" repeated Dad. And there was that look again.

Sarah rushed on. "Where are his baby pictures?"

Jake took a long time with the last button on his coat. Finally, he said, "You know, Sarah, maybe you should ask your mother about this."

"I did. She said to ask you." *Please understand, God. Please!*

"Oh," said Jake. "Well, when we moved here the movers lost some boxes. And Noah's baby pictures were in there. That's probably why she told you to see me." He grinned at

Sarah. "It still makes her mad every time somebody mentions them."

Sarah managed to smile back. "Okay. I won't say anything."

Out in the kitchen, Amy took a final sip of coffee and looked at her new partner with awe. "You've sold twenty-one houses in one week, Tess. It just isn't done!"

"Trust me, Amy." Tess smiled. "This isn't brain surgery. Now that's really hard— especially on your hands. Makes 'em cramp up."

Tess stretched her long fingers. *For all the world,* thought Amy, *like she'd really done brain surgery!* But the thought vanished as Sarah burst in. "Mom?"

Amy held up one hand. "Just a sec, Sarah."

"Oh no, you go ahead," said Tess. "I'll see you at the office."

"I won't be late," Amy said, turning to Sarah. "Something wrong, honey?"

"Kinda." Sarah hesitated. She hated doing this. "I have to make a family tree for class, and I need baby pictures."

"Baby pictures?" echoed Amy.

Sarah nodded. "There are a lot of me, but I can't find any of Noah." She watched her mother carefully.

Finally, Amy answered. "I don't know, honey . . . maybe Dad knows."

"I asked him," said Sarah in a very small, very un-Sarah voice, "but he told me to ask you."

Amy drew a deep breath, then smiled brightly as she carried her cup to the sink. "Well, all I can think of is they're probably put away somewhere."

"Put away?" repeated Sarah.

Her back to Sarah, Amy nodded. "I could look for them," she said doubtfully, "but it would take a while."

Sarah stared at her mother's shaking hands. She couldn't believe this was happening—her parents had lied to her!

"C'mon, ladies, let's go," called Jake.

"Goodness," said Amy, "where does the time go! Do you want a ride, Sarah?"

"Uh . . . no . . . no thanks." Sarah seemed to be having trouble with her zipper again. "I'll take my bike."

"Okay, sweetheart." A hug from her mother, a peck on the cheek from Dad, and Sarah was alone. She stood, frozen in place, for a long time. Then she blinked away a tear and raced upstairs.

Sarah threw open the doors to her parents' closet and stepped inside. She didn't know what she was looking for. She just knew there had to be something—anything—that would explain why her parents had lied to her. How could they? How could they!

Hands flying, she searched every rack and shelf. Finally, in a corner behind her mom's winter coat—where she'd missed it the first time—she found a flat, dusty box. 'Noah' read the label. But just as Sarah lifted the lid, the front door opened downstairs!

"I'll only be a minute, Jake," called her mother's voice. "Can't sell real estate without my blazer."

Sarah froze. How could she ever explain? As footsteps raced up the stairs, Sarah eased the closet doors closed. And held her breath. Eyes scrunched shut, she pressed back against the wall behind a row of clothes. She could hear her mother moving around the bedroom. Please let the blazer be out there! Please!

Sarah cautiously opened one eye to peek through the slats in the closet door. She pushed aside a bright blue sleeve for a better look.

Bright blue sleeve . . . ?! Oh, no! She was standing right behind the jacket her mother was looking for! And Amy was reaching for the closet door. . . .

A horn honked. Grabbing the jacket without looking, Amy called, "I'm coming, Jake!"

But, as she turned to close the closet door, she saw the dusty box in the corner. She frowned, then reached in and slid the coat back in front of it. *How did that happen?* She was always so careful. The horn honked again. "Coming!" she yelled as she ran down the stairs.

Sarah wasn't sure she'd ever breathe again. Finally, with a whoosh of air, she slid from behind the clothes and picked up the 'Noah' box.

Amy knelt in her garden and reached for another tulip bulb. The autumn sun was warm on her shoulders. She smiled happily, thinking of what her garden would look like come spring.

As Amy dug the hole for the next bulb, she thought about her day. 'The Amazing Tess' had sold another five houses!

"Hi," said a cheerful voice behind her.

Amy looked up. "Jake! You're home early."

He brushed a smudge of dirt off her nose. "I slipped out. Thought maybe we could spend some time together before the kids get home."

Amy raised her face for a kiss. "I like the sound of that." Then she frowned as she reached for another bulb. "Has Sarah seemed strange to you?" she asked.

"She's twelve, honey," Jake laughed. "She's supposed to be strange."

"Not this strange," Amy answered.

"Oh, that reminds me," he said. "I wanted to make sure we had our stories straight. Sarah asked me about Noah's baby pictures."

Amy looked up, alarmed. "She asked *you* about them. Jake, she asked me about them, too!" Then she jumped up and ran for the house.

"Amy? Amy, what's wrong?" Jake called after her.

Amy pulled open the closet doors and shoved her winter coat to one side.

"Amy?" Jake called from the hall.

"It's gone, Jake." Amy's voice shook. "Noah's box is gone!"

# Chapter

# Six

## More Questions than Answers

$A$s Monica topped the strawberry soda with a puff of whipped cream, she watched Sarah rummage through a dusty box. "Why do I get the feeling you didn't get the answers you were looking for?"

"No answers," sighed Sarah. "Just more questions."

Monica looked at the jumbled papers. "What is all this?"

Sarah shrugged as she opened a file folder. "Looks like just a lot of junk."

Monica slid the soda onto a tray. "I'll be right back," she said as she hurried to the corner booth. "How are we doing, Tess?"

"It's time to fit some of the pieces together now, Angel Girl." Tess unwrapped a straw. "Andrew and I are working on our side. Now it's up to you to take things to the next level."

Monica nodded. "All right. But how?"

Tess slid the straw into the soda. "Seize the moment, baby. Seize the moment."

"Hey!" Sarah waved a small piece of paper over her head. "Look what I found!" Monica

smiled, then turned back to Tess. But Tess—
and the strawberry soda—were gone.

"What is it, Sarah?" Monica leaned over
for a closer look.

"It's an old check." Sarah could barely sit
still. "Twenty-five thousand dollars! Wow!"

"Pioneer Legal Services," Monica read
aloud. This was it—the next piece of the
puzzle! "Sarah," she said solemnly, "this is a
lot more than just a check. It's a clue."

"Cool," said Sarah, her eyes shining.

But by the time Sarah and Monica walked
into the big office building downtown, most
of Sarah's excitement had drained away.

"Are you okay?" Monica asked gently as
they stood outside the door of Pioneer Legal
Services.

Sarah reached for the doorknob, then
pulled her hand back. "Not . . . not really."

Monica's voice echoed the questions in
Sarah's head. "Is that because you're afraid

you won't find out anything? Or because you're afraid you will?"

Sarah's voice shook just a little. "Both." Then she took a deep breath and opened the door.

They looked around the empty waiting room with the crooked pictures and dusty plants. Where was everyone? They both jumped as an inner door flew open.

A bouncy little man in a wrinkled suit rushed through, then skidded to a halt. He stared at Monica and Sarah. They were not the kind of people who usually came to his office. Still . . . a client was a client. He beamed his best smile at them and extended a welcoming hand.

"Hello, I'm Ray Bishop," he said. Then, as they walked into the office, he gestured to two chairs, "What can I do for you ladies?" he asked as they sat down.

Sarah balanced on a chair with a wobbly leg and glanced nervously at Monica. Then they both looked across the messy desk at Ray Bishop.

He cleared his throat. "My time costs three hundred dollars an hour for anything legal.

And I will absolutely not do anything illegal." Then he winked. "So, what do you need?"

"We're looking for the truth," said Monica.

Ray frowned. "What kind of truth?"

Sarah held out the canceled check. "Why did my parents give you this money?"

"All people do anymore is ask me a lot of questions," Ray muttered.

He studied the check for a long time before answering. "Well, kid, it looks like I did a job for . . ." He looked at the check again. ". . . the Monroes. And that's the truth." Then he handed it back and stood up. "Thanks for stopping by."

Ignoring the hint, Monica looked Ray firmly in the eye. "Mr. Bishop, do you handle adoption cases?"

Sarah's mouth dropped open. *Adoption!*

"I handle all kinds of cases," said Ray.

Monica continued to look him in the eye. "Would you handle the kind of adoption case in which corners are cut?"

Ray's quick "Absolutely not!" wasn't at all convincing.

"Yeah, right," said Sarah.

"Why aren't you in school?" he asked, trying to change the subject.

But Monica wasn't finished. "We need to know what happened."

"Why?" he asked.

Monica's clear eyes seemed to look right into his soul. "The truth will set you free."

Ray blinked. "That guy in the elevator . . . he said that, too." He frowned. "And then he said . . . he said he was an . . . an . . ."

Monica nodded. "Yes, he is. And so am I."

"No way," breathed Ray.

"Oh, it's true," said Monica with an angelic smile. "How else would I know about that toe you shot off so you wouldn't have to go to war in Vietnam?"

"Hey!" said Ray. "That was an accident!"

Monica's voice was stern. "Tell Sarah the truth, Ray."

Ray sank back into his chair. "All right, all right. You want the truth? Here it is. I did an adoption for the Monroes."

Sarah felt as if the floor had just dropped out from under her. "Noah isn't my brother?"

"Sorry, kid," said Ray. "Your parents should have told you."

"Where did the baby come from?" asked Monica.

But that was one question too many. "Look," he said, "this is enough truth for one day." He jumped up and opened the door. "You want to track down some missing baby, look somewhere else!"

"Oh, *I'm* not looking for him," said Monica. She nodded at Sarah, who handed him the milk carton. "His father is."

Ray stared at the picture on the carton. Then, his hands shaking, he shoved it back at Sarah. "Out! Out!" he shouted.

# Chapter Seven

## Facing the Past

Amy and Jake paced back and forth. Sarah was very late coming home from school. Where was she? And where was that box?

They spun around as the front door flew open. "Sarah! Where's the box from our closet?" Dad was really mad. He never yelled at her like that.

But Sarah had more important things to worry about. "Where's Noah?"

"Over at Billy's," Amy answered. "Sarah, did you take—"

But Sarah had questions of her own! "Why didn't you tell me about Noah?"

"What . . . what about Noah?" Her mother's eyes didn't quite meet Sarah's.

It was true. It was true! Sarah's world was falling apart. "Don't lie to me! Don't lie to me anymore! I saw Ray Bishop. I talked to the lawyer."

Jake sank down on the sofa. "You did . . . what?"

"I know all about it," said Sarah. "Noah's adopted." She brushed away her tears with an angry hand. She hated it when she cried!

Amy put her arm around Sarah and led her to the sofa. "Oh, Sarah, I'm so sorry. We wanted to tell you and Noah, but we couldn't."

Sarah sniffed. "Why not?"

Jake took Sarah's hand. "Noah came from a terrible home, honey."

"His mother used drugs," Amy told her sadly. "One day she took too many and died. And his father is in prison for a very long time."

"That's why we couldn't say anything," said Jake. "It would hurt Noah too much to know."

*Oh, Noah!* Sarah took a shaky breath. "Yeah. I guess it would. But it's different now, because Noah's father isn't in jail anymore. He's out. And he's looking for Noah!" And she pulled out the milk carton.

The looks on her parents' faces almost broke Sarah's heart. Not all mysteries were fun, she was learning. There are some questions you might not want answered.

The Monroes looked at each other and moved a little closer together on the sofa.

# Facing the Past

Across town in another living room, Grant Abbott stared at the face on the milk carton and then the original large photo near it. *Who has you, Johnny?* he thought as he leaned over and picked up the treasured photo. Slowly he ran his fingers over the glass—trying to touch the past. The photos blurred through his tears, but there was his wife, Jenna, sunlight dancing on her silky hair, smiling down at the baby in her arms. Johnny, beaming back his one-toothed smile. And himself, with his arms around them both. How happy they'd been, before . . . before . . .

Suddenly, Grant's sorrow exploded into anger! He smashed the photo to the floor. Then another and another. He raced around the room, destroying everything that reminded him of the past. Finally, breathing hard, he picked up the last photo and looked at it for a long moment. Then, with a sob, he turned and threw it across the room.

But a hand reached out and caught the silver frame, just before it hit the wall. "Good arm," said Andrew.

Grant stared at him blankly. "You're the guy from the elevator."

"Haven't there been enough things broken, Grant?" Andrew asked gently. "Hearts. Lives."

Grant turned away. He just wasn't interested . . . in the question . . . in Andrew . . . in anything. "Go away."

But going away was the last thing Andrew had in mind. Calmly, he walked over to the glowing paintings that filled the walls. "They're beautiful."

Grant sank into a chair. "Jenna did them. My wife."

Andrew nodded. "She was wonderful."

"Yes," said Grant softly, "she was." He looked at Andrew, surprised. "You knew her?"

"We met once," said Andrew quietly.

But Grant wasn't listening. His mind was in the past. "She loved painting these. They were like a window into a world all her own." Grant's eyes rested on the shimmering clouds of color. "I asked her once what they were supposed to be. And she said, 'They're supposed to be what they are.'" A smile tugged at the corner of his mouth. "That was Jenna."

Then the smile faded. "Sometimes . . . sometimes I smell her perfume. Makes me think she's here somewhere, in the other room, painting . . . feeding the baby. But then I go in and . . ."

Andrew's face was filled with compassion as he looked at Grant. Then he held out the photo he'd caught. "Beautiful boy."

Grant took it in his hands and looked down at the smiling toddler with the big blue eyes. It was the face that haunted his nights and days.

And those same eyes smiled out from the milk carton.

"Yes, he was a beautiful boy," said Grant softly. "And so sweet. He looked like Jenna. Exactly like her. . . ." He stopped. "Why am I telling you this? What are you doing here?"

"I was hoping I could make you feel better," said Andrew.

"I don't want to feel better," snapped Grant. "I don't deserve to feel better!"

Andrew shook his head. "That's not true, Grant."

"Oh yes, yes it is true!" Pain filled his voice. "Johnny and I were running errands at the mall. Johnny was laughing and playing and having a great time. And then he dropped his ball and it bounced down some steps. . . ."

Grant's voice was so soft Andrew could barely hear him. "I went after that ball. I left him and went after that ball. And when I came back . . . when I came back . . . he was gone. Gone!"

Andrew felt Grant's sorrow as if it were his own. "Grant," he said gently, "you and your son were victims of a crime. This is not your fault."

Grant shook his head. "Jenna thought it was my fault. We searched for Johnny in every way possible, but we never found him. After a while, Jenna wouldn't even look at me." His voice broke. "Then, three years after we lost Johnny, I lost Jenna in a car accident. If it was an accident."

"It was an accident, Grant," said Andrew, thinking of the loving young woman he'd taken home to heaven. "Jenna's brakes failed and she died instantly. There was no pain. And it was an accident."

Grant shrugged. There was no comfort for him in Andrew's words. There was no comfort for him anywhere. He still felt so alone. His hands tightened on the photo. "So . . . so I decided to look for Johnny again. I got his face out there again, hoping that somehow somebody would find him and bring him home. But no one has." Tears ran down Grant's face. "No one ever will."

Andrew looked at Grant with compassion, wishing the Monroes knew the truth about Noah's birth father. He was a loving man who missed his son desperately.

# Chapter Eight

## The Truth Shall Set You Free

Ray Bishop slammed his office door and carried the heavy file box down the hall. When the elevator door opened, he peeked carefully inside before stepping in. Good, no Andrew! He dropped the box on the floor, pushed the button, and stepped back—right into Andrew!

Ray jumped. "What the . . . ?"

"Hello, Ray," said Andrew. "Couldn't quite tell the whole truth, could you?"

Ray stuck out his chin. "So what are you going to do, Mr. Angel? Send me to hell?"

Andrew shook his head. "Ray, I'm not here to punish you. That's not my job. I'm here to help you and to help you help others. You're the only one who can fit all the pieces together."

Ray had no idea what Andrew was talking about. "Pieces of what?"

"The Monroe adoption," Andrew answered as the elevator came to a stop.

Ray picked up the file box. "I don't want to talk about it!"

"I know. But God wants you to," said Andrew as Ray stepped from the office elevator—*into Grant's apartment!*

"What am I doing here?" Ray squeaked.

"You're here to tell the truth." Andrew pointed across the room to Grant, asleep in his chair.

"Who's . . ." Ray's voice was as pale as his face. "Who's he?"

"That's Grant," Andrew replied. "He's the father of the boy on the milk carton. The one the young Monroe girl showed you."

Ray's face got even paler. "Oh, no. I can't do this."

Andrew shook his head. "Ray, sooner or later the truth always comes out. And this time it's sooner."

Ray gulped as Andrew woke the sleeping man. "Grant?"

Grant jumped up. "What do you want?"

Andrew nodded at Ray, who suddenly found himself talking . . . explaining. "I'm an attorney. I specialize in adoptions. . . ." Ray cleared his throat. "Seven years ago a couple came to me. They had a daughter, but couldn't have any more children. And they wanted another baby very badly. And the waiting list was very long. They heard that I . . ." Grant's eyes were making Ray very uncomfortable. He cleared his throat. "They heard that I could . . . make things happen faster. Cut through the red tape. And they could afford it. And I . . . I knew a guy . . ." He looked at Andrew nervously. "Well, anyway, he found me a little boy."

Grant stepped closer. "A little boy?"

Ray nodded. "I didn't ask any questions because I didn't want to know the answers. I just looked the other way . . . and cashed the check. I never did it again. And I haven't gone a day without thinking about it."

"Grant," Andrew said softly, "that boy was your son."

Now Grant was standing very close to Ray. Too close. "You sold my son?"

"I didn't know . . ." the little man gasped. "I didn't know he was your son!"

Grant's fists were clenched. "You knew he was somebody's son!"

Ray turned to Andrew. But there was no help there.

"Yes, he knew, Grant. But he didn't care."

Ray's shoulders slumped. "No. You're right. I'm ashamed to say, I didn't care. And I hate

that I did this, but I did it, and I can't undo it."
He hung his head. "If I could, I would."

Hope died in Grant's eyes. He let go of
Ray's jacket—the scared little man didn't
matter anymore—and turned away.

Andrew stepped in front of him. "Grant,
there's something I have to tell you. I am an
angel. I have been sent to you by God to tell
you that He is sorry this happened to you, and
He is saddened by your pain." He put his
hand on Grant's shoulder. "But I bring some
good news. Great news. Your son is alive,
Grant. And he's here!"

Grant's head lifted. "Here?"

Andrew's smile was like a celebration. "He
lives just a few miles away with a family that
loves him very much."

Grant could barely breathe. "I want to see
him. I want him back. Where is he?"

Instead of answering, Andrew turned to Ray.

Ray jumped. "Me? Oh, no, *you're* the
angel! *You* tell him."

"You're a piece of the puzzle, too, Ray,"
Andrew said kindly. "If you tell Grant where he
can find his son, you will have done your part."

Grant looked at Ray with eyes that held hope for the first time in years. "Please."

"I'll lose my attorney's license," moaned Ray.

Andrew's voice was stern. "Right now, God doesn't care about your job, Ray! This is about saving two families." Then his voice softened. "And, believe it or not, it's about saving you, too."

Ray looked up. Saving him? It was a long time since anybody—including Ray himself—had thought about that. And at that moment, Ray faced the truth. The truth about what he'd done. And not done. And had to do!

He turned to Grant. "Look, I know I can't make things right." He took a deep breath. "But I can make them better." And, as he spoke, he suddenly felt very light . . . and free.

"Yes!" breathed Andrew as the last piece of the puzzle slipped into place.

# Chapter Nine

## No Way Out

Sarah threw down her pencil. This was going to be the very worst math homework she'd ever turned in! She wished she'd never seen that milk carton!

Dad said it wasn't her fault—that a lot of people would have seen Noah's picture by now. But she still felt responsible.

Down in the kitchen, Amy and Jake discussed the problem over and over. "We'll get a lawyer," said Amy.

Jake shook his head. "It was a lawyer who did this!"

But Amy had to keep hoping. "Maybe Noah's father won't be able to find us."

"Maybe?" questioned Jake. "You want to stake all this on a 'maybe'? That man is a criminal, Amy. Do you want to come home every night wondering if he'll be standing on our porch?"

"Mom! Dad!" Noah's cheerful voice drifted down the stairs. "You forgot to tuck me in!"

"Coming, honey," called Amy, her voice only a little shaky.

Jake put his arm around her as they climbed the stairs. "It'll be okay."

"Prayers all said?" asked Amy, tucking the quilt in tight.

"Of course, Mom," said Noah. "I wouldn't forget to say good-night to God!"

Amy smiled at his indignant look. "What was I thinking!" She kissed him on the end of his nose. "Good-night, sweetheart."

"'Night, Mom." Then he frowned. "Are you crying?"

"No, honey," she answered. "I've just got something in my eye."

"Hey, pal," said Jake. "Did you have fun at Billy's house?"

Noah's eyes sparkled. "Yeah. We played on the swings and we played soldier and we had pizza. . . ."

"Sounds like a good time to me," agreed Jake.

Noah nodded, then remembered. "Wanna hear something really funny?"

"Sure," said Jake, "I can always use a good laugh."

Noah grinned. "Billy's mom. She said I look just like the boy on the milk carton." He chuckled and rolled over as the light went out.

Out in the hall, Jake turned to Amy. "Start packing. We leave in the morning."

Amy jumped as the mantel clock chimed midnight. It seemed so loud. Mustn't wake the kids! She bent to put Sarah's and Noah's baby books in the half-filled box. Now what else . . . what else?! The suncatcher! Couldn't leave Sarah's 'rainbow' behind. And Noah's paints . . . and . . . "Oh, Jake," she sighed, "how can we pack up a lifetime in one night?"

"We'll just take what we need right now, honey," he answered, "and store what we can." He put an arm around her shoulders. "We'll get through this, sweetheart."

Jake was right. They'd do what they had to do. Her answering smile was a little thin, but it *was* a smile. "I'll call Tess to sell the house for us." Her smile grew a little bigger. "That should take her about five minutes."

Jake's chuckle was worth every bit of the effort the joke took. Amy hugged him back.

"Hello, babies," came a voice from the front hall. And strolling down their staircase—in the middle of the night—came Tess.

"Tess?" This was crazy! Amy had no idea what Tess was doing there. But that didn't matter. She had to get her out. "This is really a bad time, Tess. Could it wait 'til morning?"

Tess shook her head. "No, it can't. Because when I come back, you'll all be gone. Won't you?"

"What makes you say that?" Jake tried.

One look from Tess, and he suddenly understood why people bought the house that Tess decided they should buy.

"That act won't play here, Mister," she said. "I've got a message for both of you. And the message is: If you run away from this now, you'll spend the rest of your lives looking over your shoulders."

"Who . . ." Jake cleared his throat. "Who sent this message? The father, right?"

"Yes," answered Tess, "but not the father you're thinking of. I am an angel, sent by

61

God, the Father of all fathers." As she spoke, Tess began to glow—softly at first, then brighter and brighter—until the suncatcher danced with light and painted the wall with a midnight rainbow.

Amy took a step closer to Jake. She stared at Tess. "An angel?" *Oh, how they could use an angel right now!*

But Jake wasn't as easy to convince. "Is this some kind of trick?"

"God doesn't play tricks," Tess answered. "He deals in truth. And that's what He wants to give you, if you'll stop long enough to listen."

Now Jake was mad. "There's only one truth right now. And that is that we will not let some drug-addicted convict take Noah back into some horrible life!"

Tess held up one hand. "God isn't asking you to." She looked into his angry eyes. "Jake, you're a good man, and you want the best for your family. But you are making a choice tonight that is based on a lie."

"A lie?" Jake began.

But Tess wasn't finished yet. "A lie. Noah's father was never in prison. His mother never used drugs. She did die, but in a car accident a few years after her son was kidnapped."

"Kidnapped?" Amy's voice shook.

"Noah's father is still alive," Tess told them gently. "His name is Grant. And he is a good man, too, with a heart every bit as broken as yours are."

Amy's world was falling apart. But she wouldn't let it go without a fight! "Maybe Noah has another father. But he's a stranger, Tess, a stranger. We have raised Noah. We have loved him and he loves us. He belongs with us!"

Tess shook her head. "That may be. But Noah does not belong to you, and he does not belong to his birth father. God is Noah's Father, just as He is Father to every man, woman, and child on Earth."

Amy put her head on Jake's shoulder as Tess finished. "As parents, God has trusted you to raise your children the way He wants them raised—with love and kindness for all. Not just those who share your blood, and not just those who share your house."

It was true, Amy knew. She blinked away tears. "Oh, Jake . . ."

"It's my fault," he said, facing Tess. "I heard about this lawyer who could 'make things happen' for a price. I told myself that he was just cutting through the red tape. Because . . . because that's what I wanted to believe."

But Amy knew the blame wasn't all Jake's. "We didn't ask any questions. We just looked the other way."

Tess shook her head sadly. "One man looked the other way while a child was stolen. Another man looked the other way while a child was sold. And a couple looked the other way while a child was placed in their arms."

No one answered. There was nothing to say. But there was something to do! "Seems to me," Tess said, "that it's time people stopped looking the other way and started looking to do the right thing. And you know what that is."

Amy and Jake looked at each other, holding hands like two lost children. Yes, they knew.

# Chapter Ten

## Night Visits

In the 3:00 A.M. silence a floorboard squeaked under a careless foot. The slim figure in the upstairs hall froze—breath held—in the darkness. Then the figure slowly opened the door to Noah's room, tiptoed to the bed, and pounced!

Noah's eyes flew open. "Mummmph," he tried to yell through the hand covering his mouth.

"Shhhhhh." Sarah lifted her hand. "Don't wake Mom and Dad."

"What are you doing?" squeaked Noah.

Sarah sat on the edge of the bed. "I just want you to know that it's okay that you cracked up my bike."

Noah's big blue eyes got even bigger. "It is?"

Sarah nodded. "And I'm sorry I called you all those bad words. I was mad."

"That's okay," said Noah, still waking up. Then he grinned, remembering. "And I'm sorry I told Mom you called me all those bad words, too."

"That's okay." Sarah brushed it all away with a sweep of her hand. None of that was important anymore. "And all the times you were such a pest spying on me and my friends, well, don't worry about it."

Noah couldn't believe what he was hearing. And she still wasn't finished! "And one more thing: No matter what happens," she said fiercely, "you're always gonna be my little brother. Okay?"

Noah gave a little nod. Sounded okay to him. And he sure wasn't going to argue with anything Sarah said right now. He didn't even wiggle when she hugged him.

"All right," she said, satisfied, "go back to sleep, squirt."

*'Squirt.' That sounds more like my Sarah,* he thought, drifting off.

Sarah closed Noah's door behind her, turned to go to her room, and walked right into . . .

"Monica?" Sarah gasped.

"Hello, Sarah," said her friend from the soda shop. But this Monica was . . . was glowing!

And instead of a poodle skirt and sweater, a long gown the color of sea foam drifted around her slender form.

"Are . . . are you okay, Monica?" Sarah could barely get the words out.

"Oh yes," came the smiling reply. "I'm an angel, Sarah."

"An angel?" Sarah repeated. "Like, a guardian angel?"

Monica's smile was very tender. "Just like one. And I'm here because God wanted me to make sure you were all right."

"God? You know God?"

Monica nodded solemnly. "Yes, I do."

*Uh-oh.* "Is . . . is God mad at me for what I did?" Sarah asked. "The milk carton . . . and all?"

"Not at all," Monica answered. "You sought the truth and sometimes the truth is hard to face. But you will rise above it and be freed."

Sarah was confused. "I don't know what that means."

"I know you don't," said Monica. "But God is going to help you understand."

"Can I ask you a question? About God?" Sarah never could resist a mystery.

"Of course," Monica answered.

"Can God make a rock so heavy even He can't lift it?"

Monica smiled. She loved test questions! "Let me tell you who God is. Yes, He can make a rock so heavy that even He can't lift it. And then," she said with delight, "because He is God, He can lift it anyway."

Sarah felt just a little dizzy as she thought about that. But it felt right. Of course God could do anything. But would He?

Monica understood. "You love Noah very much, don't you?"

Sarah shrugged. "He's all right. You know, for a squirt."

Monica's hand was soft on her shoulder. "Sarah, when you love someone, don't keep it a secret."

"Yes," said Sarah, "I love him. A lot."

"God knows that," said Monica gently, "and He loves Noah, too. That's why no matter what may happen here today, God will always be there for Noah. That I can promise you."

Sarah blinked back tears. She wanted to be there, too! No matter what anybody said, Noah was her brother!

"If you want to cry, Sarah," said Monica, "it's all right." She held out her arms. "Detectives cry all the time," she whispered. "They just don't tell."

Sarah stepped into Monica's waiting arms—her tears quickly getting the angel's gown very wet.

# Chapter Eleven

Moment of Truth

The soccer ball flew across the yard. "No, no!" groaned Sarah. "Like *this*, Noah. Step, step, step . . . scoop!" And finally Noah's flying feet found the ball.

Amy and Jake watched from the window, storing up memories for the time when . . . the time when . . .

"How are you two holding up?" asked Tess.

Amy managed a shaky smile. "Oh, Tess, are you sure we shouldn't tell Noah first? Before . . . before his . . . father gets here."

Tess was sure. Humans! Always ready to rush in, where even angels watched their step! "You can't jump to the second floor all at once, baby. You have to climb one step at a time. Today is just the first step."

Tess turned to the door. "I'll get it." Then, the doorbell rang.

Amy and Jake stood close together as Tess came back with two men.

"This is Andrew," she said. "He's here for me." Then she led the other man forward. "And this is Grant. He's here for you."

Time seemed to stop as Noah's parents—all of them—came face to face at last. Tess nudged Andrew. "Come on, Angel Boy, it's up to them now."

Jake's arm tightened around Amy, then he stepped forward, hand out. "Hello, I'm Jake Monroe. And this is my wife, Amy."

"Hello," answered Grant. *Hello.* Such a simple word. But it rang through the room like the end—or the beginning—of a song. For a moment no one knew what to say. Then a burst of laughter from outside put the world back on track. Grant's eyes flew to the window. "Can I see him?"

Jake cleared his throat. "He's outside with his sis . . . with our daughter, Sarah."

The walk to the window was the longest of Grant's life. Then, tears running down his face, he looked . . . and looked.

Amy's arm slid around his waist. "I thought I'd never see him again," Grant told her. "His birthday, Christmas, Father's Day . . . I'd just hold on and wait for the day to end. So I could forget. . . ."

"We've loved him like he was our own," said Amy's gentle voice.

Grant looked at her and smiled. "I can see that. Thank you."

Jake's voice was gruff. "I'll bring him in."

Amy squeezed Grant's hand. "We didn't know . . ."

He nodded. "I understand. Everything's okay now."

Jake stepped into the yard. "Noah? Come here a minute, son."

Noah scooped the ball with his foot, bounced it off his knee, and caught it! He turned to his dad with a proud grin.

"Hey, squirt." Sarah was hugging him again! "You're gonna be okay."

*What is she talking about?* Noah thought as he ran over to Jake.

"Nice moves, Noah!" said Dad. "Come inside, there's somebody you should meet."

As they heard voices in the hall, Grant turned to Amy. "I want to take this slow."

Amy nodded. "I think that's a good idea." She turned to the door. "Hi, guys."

"Hi, Mom." Noah looked curiously at Grant.

"Noah," said Jake, "this is . . . this is your . . ."

"Grant," said the smiling man with the friendly eyes. "Nice to meet you, Noah."

"Hi," said Noah. He wondered who this man was, but he knew it wouldn't be polite to ask. And Mom and Dad were very fussy about 'polite.' So he just gave Grant a big smile.

"You, ah . . . you like to play soccer?" Grant asked.

"Yeah," Noah answered.

"Me, too." Grant smiled.

Amy helped things along. "Grant is a new friend, Noah. Why don't you show him your room?"

"Sure," said Noah. "Come on, Grant." He had all kinds of neat stuff to show off.

Amy's smile lasted just until Noah and Grant were out of sight.

Sarah kicked the soccer ball aimlessly around the yard. She guessed she should go inside. But she just wanted to be alone right now. She might as well get used to it. . . .

"Oh, Sarah," said Monica, neatly catching the ball, "you're no more alone than Noah is . . . or your parents. God is with you. Always."

And the ball bounced to the ground as she held out her arms.

# Chapter Twelve

## Endings . . . and Beginnings

Wait 'til you see my room," Noah said as he held the door open for Grant. "It's really cool. And Mom doesn't even make me keep it picked up all the time. As long as," he added, checking to make sure, "there are no dirty socks under the bed."

Grant laughed, then caught his breath as he looked around Noah's room. It was filled with artwork! Joyful swirls and loops of color sang from every wall. And they were so much—so very much—like Jenna's paintings. "Did . . . did you paint these?"

"Yeah," Noah answered. "I like to paint."

Grant nodded. Of course he did. "They're very good."

"Thanks," said Noah, pleased.

"I used to know someone who liked to paint as much as you do," said Grant softly. Then he smiled at Noah. "You look exactly like your mom."

Noah shook his head. "No, I don't. She has brown hair."

Grant smiled to himself. Then he reached out and touched a painting that might be a sunrise, or the heart of a rose. . . . "Why do you paint these?" he asked softly.

"I don't know," Noah answered. "I just like to. You can have it if you want."

"Thanks," said Grant, gently touching Noah's silky hair.

"You're welcome" said Noah. He led Grant over to his desk. "Want to see the one I'm doing now?"

Noah chattered away as he picked up his brush. "It's supposed to be a surprise, but I think I'm getting some oil paints and maybe an easel for my birthday."

"In July," added Grant.

"No," said Noah, puzzled. "My birthday's tomorrow!"

Grant nodded. Noah's birthday was whenever Noah said it was. "I have lots of canvases at home. They're yours if you want them."

"Really? I can have them?" Noah beamed at Grant. "Cool, thanks! I'll make a painting for my mom and dad. They love my artwork."

Grant smiled. "That's great. You know, you're pretty lucky to have grown up here."

"Luck had nothing to do with it," said

Andrew, perched—unseen by Noah—on the corner of the desk.

*Just one more wonder,* thought Grant—returning the tall angel's smile—*in a day filled with wonders.*

Grant's step was as light as his heart, as he came downstairs. He smiled at Amy and Jake and Sarah. Then he looked thoughtfully at Tess and Monica. "Are you two . . . ?"

Tess nodded. "Uh-huh. We're with Andrew."

*Of course you are,* thought Grant.

"Grant," said Amy, "this is our daughter, Sarah."

"Hi, Sarah," he said, pleased to meet Noah's sister.

But Sarah wasn't pleased to meet him. She stuck out her chin. "Are you going to take my brother away?"

"Sarah," chorused her parents.

But Grant understood. "It's all right. This has been hard for everybody. It must have been hard for God, too, if He sent angels." Grant sat down. "I spent this morning painting Johnny's room—Johnny, that's what his mom and I named him."

80

# Endings . . . and Beginnings

Eyes on the floor, Grant seemed to be talking as much to himself as to the Monroes. "And I've been planning how to tell Johnny who I am. And I was planning all the great things Johnny and I were going to do together." He gave a shaky little laugh. "I was even planning where to send Johnny to school." He shook his head. "But God has a different plan for him. And I realize now he's not Johnny. He's Noah. He's mine and he's not. I can't take him home because he's already home."

Amy and Jake looked at each other, hope in their eyes. But Sarah—ah, Sarah!—raced right to the answer. "He's staying? Noah's staying?!" Her smile was dazzling.

Grant smiled back. "I do want him to know the truth, but not yet. In the meantime, maybe I could start getting to know him."

Grant looked at the Monroes. "I wanted him back in my family. But maybe the best way to do that is to become part of yours."

"Oh, yes," breathed Amy. She put her arms around Grant. "You are part of our family. You always have been!"

"Yes!" Tess grinned. She liked happy endings.

# Endings . . . and Beginnings

"Hey, Dad!" piped Noah from the doorway.

Jake and Grant both turned to answer. Grant smiled at Jake. "He's talking to you."

"What's up, champ?" asked Jake.

"Can Grant come to my birthday party?" Noah thought that was a really cool idea—a party and a new friend.

Jake smiled. "Why don't you ask him?"

Noah turned to Grant. "Will you?"

"I've missed too many already," was the soft reply.

Noah was puzzled. "Is that a yes?"

"That's a yes," Grant laughed.

Then Sarah did her part in welcoming Grant into the family. "Want to come outside and play soccer with us? Me and Noah against you and Dad?"

Jake turned to Grant. "What do you think?"

Grant grinned. "I think we can take 'em."

Jake laughed. "I think I should warn you: Sarah's team is city champion this year."

"Oh, no!" groaned Grant, "what have I gotten myself into?"

"We'll take it easy on you," promised Sarah. Then she turned and said, "Hey,

Monica, want to watch? Monica . . . ?" But the angels were gone.

"Who's Monica?" asked Noah.

"Never mind, squirt," said Sarah kindly. Little brothers didn't have to know everything.

Tess frowned at Andrew spinning round and round on the soda fountain stool. "Behave yourself, Angel Boy."

They both looked doubtfully at the concoction Monica placed in front of them.

"A little reward for a job well done," she beamed, adding two straws.

Oh, well . . . politeness was a virtue. They took cautious sips.

"Reward or punishment?" Tess sputtered.

"What's in this?" Andrew gasped.

"All my favorite things," came the cheerful reply. "A cherry coke, a chocolate sundae, a mocha latte . . . even a few French fries."

"Angel Girl," said Tess kindly, "some things are better together, and some things are better by themselves."

"And everything in here," Andrew added, "is better by itself!"

"And the three of us," Monica smiled, forgiving their lack of taste, "are better together."

"You've got that right," Tess agreed. "We had six hands," she added, joining hers with theirs, "and we needed every last one of them."

Then, Monica let go and reached under the counter. "Maybe a little more whipped cream."

"No!" chorused Tess and Andrew.

Too late.

A foaming cloud of whipped cream puffed into the air where it shimmered and swirled and, somehow, found wings. And a gleaming white dove lifted toward heaven.